Henry Llewellyn Williams

The Art of Boxing, Swimming and Gymnastics Made Easy

Henry Llewellyn Williams

The Art of Boxing, Swimming and Gymnastics Made Easy

ISBN/EAN: 9783337389635

Printed in Europe, USA, Canada, Australia, Japan

Cover: Foto ©Andreas Hilbeck / pixelio.de

More available books at **www.hansebooks.com**

THE ART OF
BOXING,

Swimming and Gymnastics
MADE EASY.

THE ART OF

BOXING,

SWIMMING AND GYMNASTICS

MADE EASY,

GIVING

COMPLETE AND SPECIFIC DIRECTIONS FOR AC-
QUIRING THE ART OF SELF-DEFENCE, SWIM-
MING, AND A LARGE VARIETY OF GYM-
NASTIC EXERCISES,

ENABLING ANY ONE TO BECOME AN

EXPERT BOXER AND ATHLETE.

WITHOUT THE AID OF A TEACHER,

NEW YORK :
PUBLISHED FOR THE TRADE.

THE SCIENCE OF SELF-DEFENCE;

— OR, —

THE ART OF BOXING

THE Art of Boxing has been practiced more or less among the two great nations of antiquity. The Greeks and Romans held it in high respect, and even the Jews did not wholly eschew the art of smiting, while the descendents of the Tribes who settled in England have contributed many of the most brilliant boxers to the roll of fame. That every man who desires the development of the muscular powers of the human frame, the possession of quickness, decision, endurance and courage should practice boxing as a matter of necessity, since by no other means can all these qualities be so thoroughly tested and cultivated. Every man should be able to use the weapons which nature has given him to the best of his ability—not necessarily to oppress or injure others (since the best boxers are almost invariably the least quarrelsome and overbearing persons,) but to be able to defend himself from attack or oppression on the part of others. The smallest and weakest man, by assiduous practice in boxing, may make himself an antagonist by no means to be despised; and well do we remember seeing a small, pale, slender-looking slip of a fellow, give a great hulking waterman, six or eight inches taller than himself, a very wholesome thrashing at Hampton Court once for attempting to bully him out of his fare. It was beautiful to see how the little man slipped away under the arms of the big one (who was weaving and walloping them about like the sails of a windmill,) propping him sharply here, there and everywhere, until the bully, worn-out and bleeding, admitted that he had had enough, and the little one walked off without a mark, amid the cheers of the spectators. The big one was probably careful in future to deal more carefully with his customers. Boxing has been called brutal. With persons who hold that view it is perhaps useless to argue; they look only at the worst aspect of the *means*, and entirely shut their eyes to the *object*, or better side of the question. But it may fairly be asked whether manners have improved since boxing was abolished by law; whether there is less brutality, less wife-beating and kicking, now than formerly: and whether the spectacle one so often sees, of two great hulking brutes blackguarding each other in the foulest and most filthy language, yet both afraid to hit one another from want of familiarity with the usages of combat, is an improving one? Is there less brutality, less criminal violence, often attended with fatal or nearly fatal results? less ready use of un-English and unmanly weapons and means of defence than there was formerly? We say No, emphatically, and with certainty, *no*. In the old days, when boxing flourished, if a man had been seen ill-treating a weaker one or beating and kicking a woman, twenty men who could use their fists would have come forward promptly "to help the weak," and the brute would soon have learnt at what a risk he indulged his propensities. Now, twenty men will pass by on the other side, or scuttle off down a by-street to be out of the row.

Our great fatal mistake was made in putting down what was called "prize fighting." It was *first* declared illegal, and then tolerated for many years. The professors of the art being thus placed under a social ban, and having to practice it in opposition to the law, the more respectable and better class of their patrons became gradually weeded out, and while the Tom Springs and Deaf Burkes, men of sterling worth, courage and unimpeachable honesty, passed away, worse came in their places; and then, this, the natural result of such a course of treatment was pointed to as a reason for active interference and putting fighting down altogether. Yet the native love of seeing a well *stricken* field was never so strongly displayed as when Tom Sayers and Heenan fought their well contested fight, and the best blood in England stood by the ring side and looked on with breathless interest. Had such patronage always awaited the ring, had endeavors been made to raise its status and social condition instead of lowering it; had it been recognized as a national benefit that the youth of England should know how to protect itself, should know how to bear exertion and pain with unflinching courage and endurance; had it been admitted that a school for the encouragement and practice of the art in which the highest efficiency could be obtained was a national requisite, then indeed we should have had matters placed on a different footing, and the rowdyism and blackguradism one used to hear so much of and which were mainly due to the low parasites and hangers on of the Ring would not have been heard of at all, for the professors of the art, seeing themselves respected, would have put all this down with a strong hand. As it is, the school of boxing is rapidly dying out, and when the professors of the present day have passed away it will be hard to say where the new ones are to come from. Unless, therefore, some strong step is taken to revive the fallen fortunes of the Ring, the school of British Boxing will soon be a vision of the past, and Continental manners and practices of the worst type will find a home amongst us.

USEFUL HINTS IN SPARRING.

Keep your eyes open.

Abstain from biting your lips, or putting your tongue between your teeth. Very serious accidents may occur from so doing.

The mouth ought to be firmly closed. The slightest tap on the lower jaw when it is hanging loose will be remembered for long afterwards, while a more severe blow will dislocate it. The value of this piece of advice will be the more obvious to the reader if he attempts simply to shake his lower jaw when his mouth is closed and then repeat the experiment with it open.

Endeavor in sparring to let the muscles work as loosely and easily as possible. Let all your movements be light and free. Lift the feet, do not drag them. By these means you will cultivate quickness, without which, knowledge is of little use in boxing.

In sparring round your adversary keep the left hand and foot in front of you, and after delivering a blow, work to your right, in order to get out of reach of his right hand.

Wrestling is not permitted in boxing.

It is a foul blow to hit below the belt.

Avoid if possible coming to close quarters with a man of much superior weight. In out-fighting quickness may neutralize weight, but in in-fighting the latter must always tell.

It may perhaps be as well to explain the somewhat technical expression of "in-fighting" and "out-fighting."

IN-FIGHTING means half-arm hitting, with both arms, when close to antagonist. In in-fighting a man must rely upon his quickness in hiting, and cannot pay much attention to guarding.

OUT-FIGHTNG means long-arm hitting and guard-ing, and includes manœuvring for a hit coupled with a readiness to guard.

HITTING.

POSITION OF THE HANDS AND ARMS, ETC.

In hitting make as much as possible of your weight. The blow that is simply delivered by the action of the muscles is nothing by comparison with that which is followed and driven home by the full weight of the body. Remember, also, to have the hands tightly closed. In fighting this would naturally be an unne-cessary caution; it is, however, a frequent occurence to see men hit with open gloves. Besides diminishing the force of the blow, a sprained or otherwise injured hand or wrist may follow.

In the left hand lead off at the head, the blow should be given with the upper knuckles, and in all others with the hand in the position shown in plate XXXVII.

In leading off with the *left hand at the head* the arm should be perfectly straight, with the elbow turned under and palm upwards. *Vide* plate XXXVII.

For all other blows the arm should be slightly bent, the elbow pointing outwards, and the palm turned half down and inwards. *Vide* plate XXXVII.

There are four hits, viz:

The left hand at the head.	The right hand at the head.
The left hand at the body.	The right hand at the body.

DUCKING.

DUCKING consists in throwing the head on one side and at the same time slightly lowering the body, so as to allow the blow intended for the head to pass harmlessly over the shoulder. It is an excellent method of avoiding a blow, affording, moreover, an opportunity of delivering one, for the pupil should bear in mind never to duck without at the same time hitting. When opposed to a bigger man than yourself, fight at his body, using the ducks shown in plates X and XIII.

There are five ducks.

The duck to the right, as practiced when countering with the left hand on the head. *Vide* plate XIX.

The duck to the right, when it is intended to deliver a left-hand body blow. *Vide* plate X.

The duck to the left while delivering a right-hand cross-counter. *Vide* plate XX.

The duck to the left, giving at the same time a right-hand body-blow. *Vide* plate XIII.

The duck to the right which is sometimes used when leading off at the head with the left hand, in order to avoid a counter. *Vide* plate IX.

FEINTING.

A FEINT is a false attack made to divert attention from the real danger which followd, as, for instance, a left-hand feint followed by a right-hand blow, or a feint at the head followed by a body blow. To make a feint with the left hand, straighten the arm suddenly as though you were going to deliver a blow, and at the same time advance the left foot about six inches, keeping the head back, then return to the guard.

A feint with the right hand is made thus: draw the arm back suddenly as though you were going to hit, and at the same time advance the left foot about six inches, keeping the head back, then return to the guard. "Drawing" has some affinity with feinting, and may be described under the same head. Its object is to induce your opponent to deliver a certain blow for which you are prepared, and which it is your intention to counter; you do this either by feinting and enticing him to follow you up, or by laying yourself open with apparent carelessness to the attack you wish him to make. Both are, of course, exceedingly useful, but the beginner will do well to cultivate quickness and attain some proficiency in straightforward sparring before he turns his attention to manœuvers which are more likely to get himself than his adversary into trouble if they are not preformed with great rapidity. When your opponent feints or attempts to draw you, either get back or else guard both head and body as illustrated in plate VIII.

A LEFT HAND FEINT AND LEAD OFF.

FEINT a lead off with the left hand, so as to induce your adversary to throw up his right-hand guard. Should he do so, hit at the pit of the stomach. Should he not raise his right hand, follow the feint up with a genuine lead off at the head. Particular attention should be paid in this attack to the action of the feet. Make a short step with the left foot (about six inches) as though you were going to lead off, then withdraw it and suddenly deliver the blow; using the feet as described in plates VI. and X. This movement requires some practice, as it should be performed with great rapidity.

PLATE I.
ATTITUDE.

In this position the toes of the right foot must be
directly behind and in a line with the left heel. The
distance between the feet naturally varies according
to the height; for a man of 5ft. 8in. it should be 14
inches. Let the right foot be turned slightly out, and
raise the heel about two inches from the ground; the
weight then will rest on the ball of the foot. The left
foot ought to be flat on the ground and pointed towards your opponent's left toe. Slightly bend both
knees. The right arm should be across the "mark"
(that point where the ribs begin to arch,) the hand being an inch below the left breast. To obtain the exact
position of the left arm, advance the left shoulder,
drop the arm by the side, and then raise the fore-arm
until the hand is on a level with the elbow. In sparring it should be worked easily forward and backward. Throw the right shoulder well back, and slightly sink it, so that of the two the left shoulder is the
higher. Lower the chin, turn the face a little to the
right, and bend the head slightly over the right shoulder. The object of turning the face is to prevent both
eyes being hit at once, while the head is bent to the
right in order that it may not be directly in a line
with your opponent's left hand, and thus afford him
an easy target.

THE DOUBLE LEAD OFF AT THE BODY AND HEAD.

Commence with the body blow as described in No.
X.; instead, though, of retiring immediately you have
struck out, bring the right foot about twelve inches
forward, step in a few inches with the left, and follow
the first blow up with a second aimed at the face.
Both blows, which must follow one another as rapidly
as possible, should be delivered with the left hand.
The palm in each instance ought to be turned down.

PLATE II.

SHAKING HANDS.

Both before and after a bout with the gloves, the combatants should thus salute one another. It is a good old-fashioned English custom, betokening friendly feeling and should never be omitted. A hearty shake of the hands after a warm set-to, in which both men have, perhaps, become rather more earnest than is necessary, at once dissipates what might otherwise grow into ill feeling. As the hand is extended, move the right foot to the front, and at the conclusion of the ceremony throw it smartly behind the left and assume at once the position given in plate I

PLATE III.

BOTH MEN ON GUARD.

It is of the utmost importance that a man should stand and get about well. The advantage of quick hands is sadly neutralized by slow legs. To get about quickly and safely, there must be some arrangement and method in the steps. An experienced boxer, who has paid attention to the action of the feet, always stands firmly; his feet are never flurried, the same distance usually separates them; he moves rapidly, neatly, and quietly.   With a novice, or boxer who imagines that getting about is an unimportant detail, and the manner in which he moves of no consequence, the case is different.   As a rule his movements are few and deplorably slow; when suddenly attacked, he loses his balance, and most of his attention is consequently directed to saving himself from falling. Should he, however, be more ambitious, and attempt to move with any rapidity, the whole performance is a scramble.   His feet are too close together, or too far apart, his legs are (if I may use such an expression) constantly in his way; he stumbles, staggers and rolls about in an absurd manner, not unfrequently ending by tripping himself up, and falling even without the assistance of a blow.

By referring to the plate you will see both men on guard, in the position illustrated in Plate No. I, and before proceeding further they should practice the following steps:—

To advance, move the left foot about ten inches forward, placing it upon the ground heel first.   Let the right foot follow it the same distance.   Bear in mind that the space between the feet should vary as little as possible.

To retire, step back about ten inches with the right foot, following it in like manner with the left.

To take ground to the right, move the left foot about twelve inches to the right, following it immediately with the right, and assuming again position No. I.

To take ground to the left, move the right foot twelve inches to the left, and place the left directly in front of it.

By adopting these steps the right foot is always behind the left, you are always in position, and consequently ready either for attack or defence.

PLATE IV.

BREAKING GROUND.

This is the term applied to the usual method of retreat in boxing. You break ground in the following manner. In leading off at the head your right

foot will be raised from the ground (*vide* plate VII.)
As you set it down again and the weight of the body
is transferred to it from the left leg, spring backwards.   The left foot should touch the ground first,
alighting on the same spot upon which you formerly
placed the right, which then assumes its natural position in the rear. You will thus find yourself in position a pace behind the spot from which you origi-
nally stepped in to lead off. It is necessary sometimes,
if your opponent follows you up very quickly, to double the step, that is to say, to make two consecutive
springs backwards.   For other blows, although the
right foot is not raised from the ground at the moment of striking, the movements in breaking ground
are precisely the same, for the moment the weight
falls on the right leg you spring back as described
above.

GUARD FOR **LEAD OEF** AT THE **HEAD** WITH THE RIGHT.

Raise the left elbow and bend the arm so that the
fist is somewhat lower and nearer to the body than
the elbow. Let the palm be turned to the front.
Shift the right foot back about six inches, and lean a
little forward, so that you are the better able to resist
the attack.   Look over your wrist, and receive the
blow upon the elbow.

PLATE V.

SIDE STEP.

This is exceedingly useful in avoiding a rush or
in getting away when you are driven back against
the ropes. We will suppose you to be in position facing your adversary. By a sudden movement of the

feet, half spring half step, you turn the body to the right, change the relative position of the legs, and assume the attitude of a fencer on the lunge, that is with the right instead of the left leg in front, as is usual in boxing.   Your left should now be turned towards your adversary, the line of your feet being at right angles to the line in which they formerly stood. The left foot should be upon almost the same spot formerly occupied by your right.   If your adversary advances hastily and without caution whilst you are in this posture he will be apt to trip over your left leg.   Bring the left foot into position before the right, and you will then stand a pace to the right of your original station.   If this step is executed rapidly you elude your opponent, for he will no longer be in front of you, and consequently you can easily get away from the ropes.   A combination of the side step and breaking ground should also be practiced.   Spring back as if breaking ground, and alight in the posture above described as that of a fencer on the lunge, with the body turned to the right, bring the left foot into position before the right, and you thus get back and work to the right of yourself at the same time.

LEFT-HAND COUNTER ON THE BODY.

This should be delivered when your adversary is leading off at your head with his left hand.   Duck to the right, step in about twelve inches, and aim your blow at the pit of his stomach.   The right hand should be drawn seven or eight inches back, and held close to the side.   To get away, turn the left heel out and spring well back.   Do not raise the head until out of distance.

PLATE VI.

LEFT-HAND LEAD OFF AT THE HEAD WITHOUT GUARDING.

The lead off at the head should, as a rule, be made with the left hand. Its importance can hardly be exaggerated. Every effort should, therefore be directed towards attaining proficiency in this particular. A quick lead off frequently enables a man to score

point after point without receiving a return.   He
spars round his adversary, watching for an opportunity, and then, having measured hisd istance well, steps
in, plants a blow, and is away again at once.   With
these tactics at his command, a light man will often
fight a heavy weight all over without coming to close
quarters, at which weight would inevitably tell in fa-
vor of its possessor.   A slow lead off lays a man open
to counters and cross-counters, which will hereafter
be described.

The lead off should be made when the hand is in
the position shown in plate No. I.   In all other blows
the hand is more or less drawn back before delivery;
in this case, however, it should come straight out, as
it were, spontaneously, and without the slightest hes-
itation.   Beginners are almost always inclined to hit
downwards, or "chop" and bear heavily upon their
opponent's guard.   This should be avoided.   In stepping in push yourself off the ball of the right foot,
and spring in about eighteen inches.   The action of
foot and arm should be simultaneous; do not step in
and then deliver the blow.   The lead off at the head
with the left hand is the only blow that is delivered
while the right foot is raised from the ground.

As you step in the right foot should follow, and,
at the moment of striking, hang over the spot formerly occupied by the left.   Full advantage is thus
taken of height and reach.   Be careful when you step
in to place the left foot upon the ground, heel first.
If the toe touches the ground first, and your adversary by chance gets back instead of guarding or receiving your blow, you do not meet with the expect-
ed resistance, and consequently are apt to overbalance;
in which case, until you can recover yourself, you are
at his mercy.   The head and right hand remain in
position No. 1.

PLATE VII.

RIGHT-HAND GUARD FOR THE HEAD,

To guard the head from your opponent's left hand, raise the right hand nearly to a level and in front of the left temple.   Let the fore-arm cross the face, and be thrown forward so as to turn instead of receiving the weight of the blow.   Keep the elbow down. Close the hand firmly in order to brace the sinews, and turn the palm partly outward or the blow will fall on the bone of the arm instead of the muscle.   At the same time bend the head forward and to the right—thus, although the face is well out of danger, you can still see your opponent over the fore-arm.

PLATE VIII.

LEFT-HAND LEAD OFF AT HEAD AND GUARD.

The lead off in this case is precisely the same, but, at the moment of hitting, you also throw up the right hand guard to protect the face from a possible left hand counter.   It requires a little practice to do this without detracting from the rapidity of your lead off; your trouble will, however be well spent, for with an opponent who frequently attempts left-hand counters this will be found a very useful manœuvre.

For the feint of this lead off, *see* p. 12.

PLATE IX.

LEFT HAND LEAD OFF AND DUCK.

This illustration represents the same lead off again. In place of the right-hand guard, it is, however, accompanied with a duck, thus avoiding instead of guarding the left-hand counter. Observe that for this blow the right foot is not raised; it does not follow the left as in the preceding examples, but remains firmly planted on the ground, as in the left-hand body blow.

PLATE X.

LEFT-HAND BODY BLOW.

This blow should never be attempted unless you are confident that you have sufficient room behind you to be able to get well away again. It should be directed at the pit of the stomach, which is the weakest part of the body. Occasionally it may with advantage be preceded by a feint at the head, in order to induce your opponent to throw up his right hand guard and lay the "mark" open. Let the ball of the right foot be kept well on the ground. Step in about thirty inches with the left foot, hitting out at the same time and ducking to the right. In the event of your adversary attempting to counter you with the left, your head will thus be outside his arm, which will pass harmlessly over your left shoulder. For this blow the arm should be slightly bent, the elbow turned out, and the palm of the hand turned inwards and partly down. The right arm should in the meantime be drawn back seven or eight inches, and the glove held close to the side. To get away, turn the left heel outwards and spring well back, taking care not to raise the head until out of distance.

PLATE XI.

STOP FOR LEFT-HAND BODY BLOW.

Like all stops, this requires very accurate timing. Having forseen your adversary's intention, hit him full in the face with your left hand before he can get his head down. Keep your right arm in its original position across the "mark." .

PLATE XII.

GUARD FOR LEFT-HAND BODY BLOW.

It is customary, in order to prevent the preceding "double," to cover both body and head at the same time. When, therefore, the body is attacked, put up the right hand guard, and, at the same time, throw the left arm well across the "mark" (*vide* plate VII.) Be careful to hold it firmly against the body, for even the jar of a severe body blow will knock a good deal of the wind out of a man. Step back about six inches with the right foot, so as to be the better able to resist a rush.

This is also a guard for double lead off at body and head described on p. 15.

PLATE XIII.

RIGHT-HAND BODY BLOW.

This should be aimed at a little below the heart.
It is delivered under the same circumstances and in
the same manner as the left-hand body blow (*vide* No.
X.,) with these exceptions: You duck to the left instead of right, and the feet when you have stepped in
should only be twenty inches apart instead of thirty;

you have consequently to get nearer your opponent before attempting it. Be sure always that you have sufficient room behind you for retreat.

Should he attempt to put his left arm around your neck while you are delivering this blow, duck to your right under his arm and get away. This should always be done when a man attempts to seize your head. When opposed to a man who stands with the right leg in front, you must duck to your left.

PLATE XIV.

STOP FOR RIGHT-HAND BODY BLOW.

This stop is exactly the same as that recommended for the left hand body blow. *Vide* No. XI,

PLATE XV.

GUARD FOR RIGHT-HAND BODY BLOW.

Bring the left side forward and drop the left arm, which should be slightly bent, so as to cover the side and front of the thigh. Care should be taken to press the arm close to the body, in order to prevent the jar through which you would otherwise feel much of the force of the blow,

PLATE XVI.

A LEAD OFF AT THE HEAD WITH THE RIGHT, AND GUARD FOR IT.

Feint with the left, hitting your opponent on the right arm.   Do not withdraw your hand, but as he raises his guard rest upon it with your left and pin it to his chest; then bring in the right hand, aiming it at the chin or angle of the jaw.   Properly delivered this is a most punishing blow, for by steadying your-self with the left hand you can bring your full force into play with the right.

For guard for lead off at the head with the right, see p. 20,

PLATE XVII.

LEAD OFF WITH RIGHT HAND AT HEAD, AND DUCK.

When leading off at the head with the right, you
may duck to the left, and avoid a right-hand counter.
In this illustration both men are preforming this manœuvre.

PLATE XVIII.

LEFT-HAND COUNTER ON THE HEAD.

This happens when two men lead off at the head with the left hand at the same time.

PLATE XIX.

LEFT-HAND COUNTER ON THE HEAD, AND DUCK.

There are, perhaps, few blows more unpleasantly startling than a good left-hand counter which meets you full-face. It opens a spacious firmament to the bewildered eyes, wherein you discover more new planets in a second than the most distinguished astronomer ever observed in a life-time. As your adversary leads off at your head with his left hand, duck to the right so as to allow his blow to pass over your left shoulder; step in about twelve inches and strike out at his face. The right foot should not be moved. Here both men have, as it happens, made use of the same stratagem; in consequence of which, both left arms have passed harmlessly over each other's left shoulder.

_____

LEFT-HAND COUNTER ON THE HEAD AND GUARD.

The difference between this and the preceding counter will be easily understood by studying the plate. It consists simply in guarding your opponent's lead off instead of ducking to avoid. You step in and hit out as before.

PLATE XX.

RIGHT-HAND CROSS COUNTER.

This is the most severe blow which can be dealt in sparring. It is delivered as follows: As your opponent leads off at your head with his left hand, step in about twelve inches, ducking to the left, at the same time shooting your right hand across his left arm and shoulder. The blow should be aimed either at the angle of the jaw or chin, and the palm of the hand should be half turned down. Let both feet be turned slightly to the left, as by these means the right side is brought forward and greater force given to the blow. As the counter is delivered, draw the left hand back to the position illustrated in the plate, then, should a second blow be necessary, before getting away you can deliver it.

PLATE XXI.

STOP FOR RIGHT-HAND CROSS COUNTER.

Anticipating your adversary's intention, hit him full in the face with the left hand before he ducks; or, instead of striking at his face, deliver the blow on the right side of his chest near to the shoulder, and his right hand will be effectually stopped.

ANOTHER STOP FOR RIGHT-HAND CROSS COUNTER.

As you lead off with your left drop the head well forward, so that at the end of the movement your left ear will be touching the inside of your upper arm when the angle of your jaw and chin will be completely covered by your shoulder.

Body blows with left or right hand will act as stops for all right hand hits at the head.

For left-hand counter on the body, see p. 22

PLATE XXII.

RIGHT-HAND COUNTER.

This occurs when both men lead off together with the right hand,

PLATE XXIII.

STOP FOR RIGHT-HAND COUNTER.

Duck your head to the left as you lead off.

RIGHT-HAND COUNTER ON THE BODY.

Dtck to the left in order to avoid your opponent's lead off, and strike out with the right hand at a point a little below the heart. The left hand should be drawn back as shown in the illustration. In all other particulars this blow represents the preceding. For this and the left-hand counter, it will be well to study the right and left hand body blows (Nos. XIII. and X,) for, with the exception of the circumstances under which they are delivered, and the difference in the distance of the advance made the blows are the same,

PLATE XXIV.

LEFT-HAND UPPER CUT.

This blow, which in reality is a counter, should be given when a man is leading off at your head with his left hand holds his head down.   Guard your face with the right arm, step in about twelve inches, and hit upwards with the left.   The arm should be bent and elbow turned down.   The force of the blow must come in a great measure from the body.

PLATE XXV.

DRAW AND STOP FOR LEFT-HAND UPPER CUT.

Feint a lead off at your opponent's face with your head down, then duck to the right, and give the left-hand body blow as described in No. X.

PLATE XXVI.

RIGHT-HAND UPPER CUT.

With this exception that you do not guard, this blow is similar to and delivered under the same circumstances as the left-hand upper cut. In delivering it the head should be slightly bent to the left.

PLATE XXVII.

A DRAW AND STOP FOR RIGHT-HAND UPPER CUT.

Feint with the head as if it were your intention to lead off with it down, then throw the head back and lead off at your adversary's face with the left hand.

PLATE XXVIII.

ANOTHER DRAW AND STOP FOR RIGHT-HAND
UPPER CUT.

Feint a lead off at your opponent's face with your left hand, then duck to the left and put in the right-hand body blow.   The reader should notice in this, as in other illustrations, the position of the hand not absolutely in use.   Never drop your hands until out of distance.

PLATE XXIX.

HOW TO PREVENT YOUR ANTAGONIST FROM HITTING
AFTER YOU HAVE LED OFF AND PASSED OVER
HIS LEFT SHOULDER.

When this occurs, bend the elbow quickly, place
your fore-arm against his throat, and thrust his head
back.   Grasp his left shoulder with your left hand
and seize his left elbow with your right hand.   This
will effectually stop him from hitting you.

PLATE XXX.

SLIPPING.

This is an exceedingly useful manœuvre, which enables you to avoid a rush or get out of a corner. Feint a lead off, tapping your adversary lightly on the chest or right arm; do not then retire, but as he comes at you duck to the right, make another step forward (as described in the lead off with a double step in,) and pass under his left arm.   To face him again, turn to the left,

PLATE XXXI.

THE HEAD IN CHANCERY.

No directions can be given for getting a man into this position. When in close quarters, you should, however, always be on the look out for a chance of doing so. If it occurs, grasp your opponent firmly around the neck with the left arm and use the right to punish him.

PLATE XXXII.

TO-GET OUT OF CHANCERY.

Almost the best advice to give a man who is firmly and fairly caught in chancery is not to attempt to get out, at least unless the hold loosens, and he can make his effort with some chance of success.   In pulling away or resisting he is simply hanging himself.   He should, therefore, push his opponent back (see plate XXXI,) and at the same time fight to the best of his ability with both hands.   If, however, he discovers the danger before the grasp has tightened, he should place one hand under his adversary's fore-arm near the elbow, the other under the shoulder, and push the arm up, ducking at the same time, and dragging the head away.

PLATE XXXIII.

IN-FIGHTING.

In-fighting generally takes place in a corner or
near the side of a ring.   In in-fighting bring the right
foot forward until it is nearly in a line with the left,
drop the chin and lean forward, so as to receive the
blows on the forehead. Keep your eyes fixed on your
antagonist.   Use both hands and hit rapidly, bringing
the shoulder well forward at each blow.   The arms
should not be drawn too far back, as time is lost there-
by; a great deal of the force of the blow is obtained by
turning the body slightly to right or left as you hit. It

is a great advantage to have your hands inside your
opponent's, you should, therefore, keep them as close
together as possible, so as to obtain, or if you already
have it, keep this advantage.   Aim the left hand at
the eyes and nose, the right at the chin or angle of the
jaw.   After delivering five or six blows, get away.
Never fight at the body in in-fighting, invariably make
the head your mark.

PLATE XXXIV.

TWO MEN ON GUARD, ONE WITH LEFT AND THE
OTHER WITH RIGHT LEG IN FRONT.

PLATE XXXV.

GUARD FOR RIGHT-HAND LEAD OFF AT HEAD WHEN
OPPOSED TO A MAN WHO STANDS WITH RIGHT
LEG IN FRONT.

PLATE XXXVI.

DUCK AND COUNTER FOR A LEAD OFF AT HEAD BY
A MAN WHO STANDS WITH RIGHT LEG IN FRONT.

———————

THE WAY TO DEAL WITH A MAN WHO STANDS WITH
HIS RIGHT LEG AND RIGHT ARM IN FRONT.

Work to your left in order to avoid his left hand.
Be chary in leading off with the left hand, as that is
at once difficult and dangerous.   It is far better to
lead off with the right hand and duck at the same

time to the left. When your adversary leads off with the right hand, duck to the left and counter either upon the face or body.

The blow on the face must be given like the right cross counter (*vide* plate XX.,) and the one on the body like the right-hand body blow shown in plate XIII., except that you must aim at the pit of the stomach instead of at a little below the heart.

THE GUARDS FOR AN OPPONENT WHO STANDS WITH

HIS RIGHT LEG IN FRONT.

When he leads off with the right-hand guard with the left arm as shown in plate XXXV, guard his left with your right arm, as shown in plate VII.

Use the guards, illustrated in plates XV and XII, for his right and left hand body blows, guarding his right with your left and his left with your right.

Avoid in-fighting with him as much as possible.

I have now, to the best of my ability, described the principal hints, stops, guards, &c., in boxing, as I use and teach them myself. Having to a certain extent perfected himself in these, the pupil will do well to go through the following exercises, making the hits as smartly and as rapidly in succession as possible, but not omitting to return to the position illustrated in plate No. I, after each blow. The opponents should take it in turns to guard and attack.

First Exercise.

1.—Left-hand body blow (get back.)
2.—Right-hand body blow (get back.)
3.—Left hand lead off at the head, guarding with the right (get back.)
4.—Right-hand cross counter (get back.)
5.—Lead off at the head with the left and duck to the right (get back.)

Second Exercise.

1.—Right hand body blow (get back.)
2.—Lead off with the left at the head without guarding (get back.)
3.—Right-hand cross counter (get back.)
4.—Left-hand body blow (get back.)
5.—Lead off with the left at the head and duck (get back.)

Third Exercise.

1.—Lead off with the left hand at the head without guarding (get back.)
2.—Right-hand cross counter (get back.)
3.—Left-hand lead off at the head and duck to the right (get back.)
4.—Left-hand body blow (get back.)
5.—Right-hand body blow (get back.)

FOURTH EXERCISE.

1.—Lead off with left at body, then make a short step in and repeat the blow on the face (get back.) (*This is the double lead off at body and head*, vide *page* 8.)
2.—Lead off with left and right at head (get back.)
3.—As your opponent retires, advance quickly, then step in and deliver the left on the face (get back.)
4.—Both men lead off with left and guard (get back.)

FIFTH EXERCISE.

1.—Lead off with the left hand at the head (get back.)
2.—Right-hand cross counter, remain and commence in-fighting, deliver five or six blows and get back.

Never degenerate into a rough, unmeaning, un-scientific scramble. In the midst of impetuosity remember coolness; and never let the heat of action lead you to forget good-temper. Be manly; seek no undue advantage. Science and pluck give advantage enough.

LEFT HAND LEAD OFF AT HEAD.

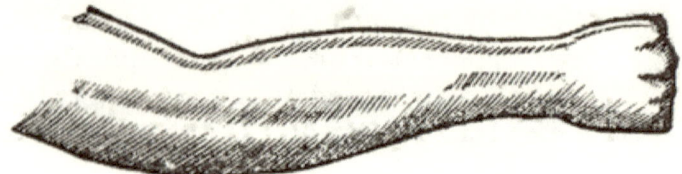

RIGHT-HAND CROSS COUNTER.

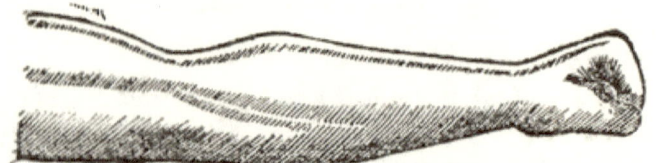

LEFT-HAND BODY BLOW.

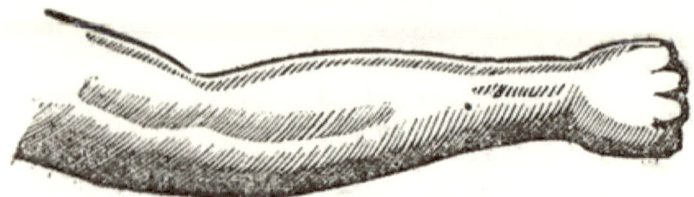

RIGHT-HAND BODY BLOW.

PLATE XXXVII.

POSITIONS OF THE HANDS WHEN HITTING.

BOXING COMPETITIONS.

There is no published code of rules for the management of boxing competitions or for the guidance of the judges, so I beg to offer the following suggestions, which may be of service until a proper set has been formed by some recognized authority.

In boxing competitions, there should be four judges, a referee and timekeeper; a judge to sit at each corner of the ring (outside,) and the referee to move about so that he may see the whole of the manœuvring and hitting, and at the end of each round the referee and judges should assemble and decide, during the interval between the rounds, which man has had the advantage. When the judges sit together, they cannot possibly see all the hits given.

The competitors should toss for corners.

The referee should under no circumstances be the timekeeper, as he cannot both keep time and watch the rounds.

In judging, both body and head blows, indeed, all points in boxing should be taken in consideration, as well as form and style.

In-fighting should not be ignored and looked upon as roughing. There is great art in it, and in a street fight it is much more useful than out-fighting.

The competitors should be divided into four weights, termed "Feather," "Light," "Middle" and "Heavy," viz:—

Feather for men under 112 lbs.

Light   "   140 lbs.

Middle   "   158 lbs.

Heavy for men of any weight.

Three rounds should be sparred, the first and second of three minutes duration each, and the third of four minutes. A minute allowed between the rounds.

On time being called, the men should go into the middle of the ring and begin the round and continue it, unless an accident should happen, until the judges stop them.

No wrestling, kicking, hitting below the mark, butting, striking with the elbow or palm, or taking hold of the hair should be permitted any man willfully doing any of the above, should be first cautioned, and upon a repetition, disqualfied by the judges.

In striking the blow *must* be delivered with the hand closed.

The seconds should not be allowed to be in the ring except during intervals between the rounds, neither should they be permitted to direct their men during a round, either by word or sign.

When a competitor draws a bye, he should invariably be compelled to spar three rounds of the same duration as the others.

No competitor should be allowed to lay hold of the ropes to assist him in the contest.

Any competitor who may be disabled during a round, and not be able to renew the contest before sixty seconds have expired, shall be considered beaten.

HOW TO PITCH A RING.

The ground should be level, and where there is sufficient room the ring should be 24 feet square, formed of two lines of ropes and eight stakes.

The stakes should be strong, with round tops, and have holes or rings through which to run the ropes, and should be firmly fixed in the ground, out of which they should stand 5 feet.

Two rows of ropes of 4 inches in circumference should be run around the ring, the bottom one about 2 feet 3 inches from the ground, and the top one 4 feet 3 inches.

When the ring is on a raised stage, a stout piece of wood about 5 or 6 inches deep should be fixed all around the edge of the floor to prevent the men slipping off.

Under no circumstances should the ring be less than 12 feet square. In a ring of less dimensions the men would not have sufficient room to use their feet withou' which there can be no good boxing.

WINNERS

—OF—

THE MARQUIS OF QUEENSBERRY'S

BOXING CHAMPIONSHIP CUPS

Since the Commencement of the Competitions.

HEAVY WEIGHTS.

1867.	J. C. HALLIDAY.	1873.	F. B. MADDISON.
1868.	T. MILVAIN.	1874.	D. GIBSON.
1869.	No competition.	1875.	A. L. HIGHTON.
1870.	H. J. CHINNERY.	1876.	R. WAKÉFIELD.
1871.	H. J. CHINNERY.	1877.	J. M. R. FRANCIS.
1872.	E. B. MICHELL.	1878.	R. FROST SMITH.

MIDDLE WEIGHTS.

1867.	H. J. CHINNERY.	1873.	A. WALKER.
1868.	H. J. CHINNERY.	1874.	F. R. THOMAS.
1869.	H. J. CHINNERY.	1875.	J. H. DOUGLAS.
1870.	E. B. MICHELL.	1876.	J. H. DOUGLAS.
1871.	E. C. STREATFIELD.	1877.	J. H. DOUGLAS.
1872.	H. J. BLYTH.	1878.	G. I. GARLAND.

LIGHT WEIGHTS.

1867.	R. CLEMINSON.	1873.	C. T. HOBBS.
1868.	No competition.	1874.	L. DENEREAZ.
1869.	H. L. JEYES, W. O.	1875.	H. S. GILES.
1870.	R. V. CHURTON.	1876.	A. BULTITUDE.
1871.	R. V. CHURTON.	1877.	H. SKEATE.
1872.	R. V. CHURTON.	1878.	G. AIREY.

POINTS TO BE OBSERVED.

" Begin with gentle toils, and as your nerves
Grow firm, to hardier, by just steps aspire."

HAVE a motive ! If possible in walking, jumping, climbing,
or in doing any of the exercises given in this Treatise, have a
motive and a will. A companion will sometimes add a zest to
what would otherwise be a dull and listless mode of passing the
time or fulfilling a duty. It is for this reason that games are
so much more beneficial as a branch of physical education,
than the best designed system of exercise, or other appliance.
Winter, spring, and summer generally bring some seasonable
enjoyment with them, which should be eagerly embraced as an
adjunct to the exercises here given. The increased bodily vig-
or will greatly assist the enjoyment of all. Golf, cricket,
sliding, skating, digging, gardening, dancing, all give vigor and
action to the human frame, and employ the mind as well as the
body.

Attention should be paid to the regularity of breathing.
Whatever increases the capacity of breathing improves the
health, and the greatest attention is given to this point by all
gymnastic teachers. Good wind is necessary for all feats—for
the enjoyment of outdoor exercise of every description. It may
be wonderfully improved by reading aloud, by taking long in-
spirations on first rising in the morning, either indoors or
before an open window, or, better still, in a garden, at first
cautiously, but it may be continued for ten minutes at a time.
Few things are better as a guard against consumption, and for
improving the breathing generally.

The dress, too, must be considered. It should be loose
fitting, and, if possible, of flannel, confined with a belt round
the waist. Taste will dictate the color, and convenience the
width of the belt. The shoes should be of soft leather, light,
and made like Irish "brogues," without heels.

Sudden transitions are to be avoided. Exercise to be of use
should begin gently and terminate in the same manner. The
left hand and arm should be exercised until they become strong

like those of the right. Beware of draughts ; being cooled too quickly when perspiring is injudicious. Drinking while hot and getting into a cold current of air must be avoided. A coat or wrapper should be handy to cover over the body the moment exercise is over. No exertion should be carried to excess, as that only exhausts the body. Strength will come surely and gradually.

Economize your power. Do not waste your energies. Avoid kicking with your legs when performing a feat with your arms and hands. Do what you have got to do quickly and easily. The best gymnasts are those who perform their feats with the least effort.

FREE MOVEMENTS.

"If at first you don't succeed,
Try again."

Good resolutions are made at night and broken in the morning. It is tiresome to think how we must be roused from our sleep to undergo a course of active exercise, and begin those horrid gymnastics. But you can begin, my trembling boy, in bed. Poor dyspeptic, you may begin by

Exercise 1.—Lay yourself on your back in bed, if you like, but the floor is better. Keep the body stiff, and let your arms lie close to your sides. Legs and heels to lie in the same line. Now, without moving the heels, raise the body perpendicular from the hips upwards, without moving your legs. How strange you could do it so easily ! Lie down and try again. Better done this time. Just cross your arms over your breast, and "try again." Practice this ere you rise, varying it by clasping the hands over the head, and raise the body as before, keeping the arms on a line with the shoulders. This is a practical illustration of domestic gymnastics, which you may try before you rise.

Exercise 2.—Try and raise the right leg, until it is perpendicular. Now lower it again by raising the body until it rests by the side of the other. Try the same movement with the left leg. When you can do this easily, try both together. Rather funny, is't it, to have a gymnastic lesson in bed? When your back will bear the strain, endeavor to raise the lower extremities and pelvis so as to touch the pillow behind your head with your toes. This is not difficult, and on a hard mattress is excellent practice for the muscles of the posterior portion of the human frame. Keep the arms extended, resting on the mattress, the knees stretched. Return gradually to your old position, and you will find yourself quietly seated on the floor. Now vary the movement by sitting up, bend the knees, lay the soles of your feet flat against each other. Extend your arms, and hold the lower part of your legs steadily between your hands. Lower yourself on your back ; carry your legs over your heels ; keep your arms full extended ; make a slight contrary movement, and return to your original position. If you prefer it, you may try

Exercise 3.—Turn your face to the mattress (for of course you are not so effeminate as to sleep on a feather bed), and extend yourself longitudinally, supporting yourself by the strength of your arms and toes ; [see Fig. 1] the hands must be turned inward and the fingers point toward each other. Now allow the body to sink slowly, let the arms bend gently, still keeping the body extended, without permitting the stomach to rest. Touch the hands with the lips and return slowly to the first position. Repeat the movement deliberately again and again. A very useful variation may be thus performed. While in the foregoing position (Fig. 1.), put the right hand under the right hip, leave the left hand in its place as before. Allow the body to sink, gently bend the arms, keep the body still extended on the toes, touch the left hand with the lips, and return to first position and restore the right hand to its place. Repeat the movement with the left hand under the left hip, and you will have exercised many of the most important muscles of the body. Now you may get up, and recollect that your lungs have been lying all night breathing slowly. Remember they are like a bladder in their structure, and can be stretched open to double their ordinary size with perfect safety. Expand the chest and defy consumption. On rising from the bed place yourself in an erect posture, throw your chest forward and your shoulders entirely off your chest. Now take a long inspiration, suck in all the air you can—inhale nature's universal medium, the common air, so as to fill your lungs. Hold your breath, throw your arms behind, holding your breath as long as possible. Now for the sponge-bath, if a shower-bath is not handy ; rub yourself dry with a coarse towel—don t be afraid of a little friction—and we will then proceed. When we come to deal with apparatus, we shall have something to say of a chest expander which may be used with advantage in the early morning in the bedroom.

Before the gymnast proceeds further with his morning exercise, a draught of water and a crust will assist him materially. He may then try

EXERCISE 4 (Fig. 2).—This is a very simple movement. The body is placed upright, with the feet together. [See Fig 2.] The arms are extended and the body thrown on alternate sides (as shown in the above diagram) until the hands nearly touch the floor. This exercise will be found useful in all cases where any ill habit or contraction has been acquired by sedentary habits, as a consequence of wrong positions in sitting, writing. sleeping ; or where there is some natural inclination to deformity. The exercise may be continued with any degree of force, and varied according to the strength of the pupil.

EXERCISE 5.—By this time the pupil will have acquired a knowledge of what muscles he has, and of what use he can make of them. Simple as the exercises have been, it will be found that some of the muscles are stiff and not easily moved, yet it will soon wear off, and the pupil will rejoice in the freedom of his limbs. He may now proceed to the "extension" movements, as depicted in Fig. 3. Place the feet close together

and the toes across a straight line, so as to mark the situation
of the feet; place the hands by the side; elevate them quickly
above the head, and bring them forcibly and energetically
down. [See Fig. 3.] Close the hands, palms upwards, and
bring the fists close to the shoulders. Drive them forth, as if
into your inveterate enemy, and then bring them back until
your hands are level with your sides. Repeat each movement
again and again—up, down, forward, backward. This exercise
is useful to old and young, and possesses the advantage of
being resorted to in all times and places, and brings into play
the thoraic, dorsal, and abdomidal muscles.

Exercise 6.—Stand as in Fig. 3. Stretch out the hands
straight at the shoulders before the body, and place the palms
of the hands together. Now slowly seperate the hands, keep
them at the same level, the arms straight, and try to make the
backs of the hands meet behind you. This, to all, at the commencement, seems to be impossible; yet as the chest expands
it becomes perfectly easy, though at first it will make the
shoulders and chest rather stiff.

Exercise 7.—Stand in the same position [Fig. 4.] Grasp
the left hand with the right, bring the arms behind the head,
and move them from one side to the other. This brings the
pectoral muscles into play with those round the shoulder.

Exercise 8.—Stand as before. Place the hands behind and
let the palms touch, with the fingers pointing downwards as in
Fig. 5. Now turn the fingers inward, and bring the hands as
high as possible up the back, taking care to keep the palms of
the hands close together. [See Fig. 6.]

Exercise 9.—Position as before. Close the hands, draw the
elbows back until the hands touch the sides, and move them
backwards and forwards until they move easily. You may now
try the circular movement, as in Fig. 7, which is one of the
best methods of enlarging the capacities of the air cells of the
lungs. You may strike the palms and wrists together as they

pass in front. Every one of these exercises can be done in a bedroom, parlor, or study.

EXERCISE 10.—Stand as before ; bring the arms quickly in front as high as the shoulders. [See Fig. 8.] Turn the nails upwards, then swing them forcibly backwards, at the same time turning the nails backward. Keep the body perfectly upright. Do this slowly many times. Stretch the arms out as in Fig. 8, and place the palms together, keep the arms at same level, and bring the hands behind you, and try to make them meet [See Fig. 9.] This movement ought to be tried night and morning, until the hands touch easily.

EXERCISE 11.—A very powerful method of giving full play to the muscles of the chest, is here represented· Bring the right hand to the left shoulder. Extend the left arm on a line with the shoulder, [Fig. 10]. Throw the right arm by the right side, place the left arm on the right shoulder, and change the positions alternately several times. Then proceed to Fig. 11. Open the hands, raise the arms sideways, and touch the back of the hands straight over the head.

The foregoing exercises all more or less tend to exercise the muscles of the arms, chest, neck, and to give free play to the respiratory organs ; they may be varied in their order, or alternated with any of the following, which call other muscles into play, producing at first, in some instances, a painfully delightful sensation.

EXERCISE 12.—Amongst the old "extension" motions taught to our soldiers, are two which find an appropriate place here. The first practice is to stand upright, with the heels together, raise the arms straight upwards, the palms in front. Bend the body forward, as shown in the annexed sketch, until the fingers touch the ground. The knees must be kept straight. [See Fig. 12.] This must be practised until a coin can be picked up with ease at each heel.

EXERCISE 13.—Take a staff or stick about three and a half

feet long. Grasp each end firmly over by the hands, with the end of the fingers towards the body, now raise the stick over the head, keeping the elbows straight, and hands firm until the stick touches the thighs. This is a very severe but excellent exercise.

EXERCISE 14.—Before you commence the following movements, strengthen the toes by raising the body on them with a stiff leg and straight knees as high as possible [Fig. 12.] Do it slowly, again and again; vary it by stepping from the toes, jumping from toes, keeping the knees straight and the body upright. Place the hands on the hips, left leg in front, toe towards the ground, and jump forward on the right toe. [See Fig. 14.] Use both legs alternately.

EXERCISE 15.—This will prove a somewhat difficult exercise at first, and will require the muscles of the legs and hips to be powerfully exerted. As you stand upright, lift the left foot behind, bend the right knee, lower the body gradually until you touch the ground with the left knee. Rise again; do it slowly with each leg in succession.

EXERCISE 16.—Stand upright as before. Extend the right arm at a right angle with the body, attempt to kick the hand with the right foot. It cannot be done at first, and may be tried with each leg and foot successively. The exercise may be varied by attempting to kick the back of the thigh with the heels alternately and rapidly. A third variation of the kicking practice, is to kick the chest with the knee, care being taken that the body is upright and the chest is not bent forward. When proficient in these exercises, try to kick both thighs together with both heels simultaneously. To perform the last feat well, a slight spring will be required. Both feet must come down on the same spot, and the performer ought not to lose his balance.

EXERCISE 17.—Place both feet together, and the hands on the hips. Kneel slowly until both knees rest on the ground,

Rise again without removing the hands from the hips, or the toes from a given line. Vary this by crossing the toes. Bend the knees gradually until you sit down a la Turk. Rise again without moving the hands from the hips. Very hard this.

EXERCISE 18.—You have probably found your level ere you have become proficient with the foregoing. Close your feet, extend your arms in front, bend the right knee gradually, and sit down in the same position. Try both legs alternately. This feat will at first seem a poser, but it is not so impossible as it at first appears.

EXERCISE 19.—This is a pleasant amusement both for old and young, and if done properly, calls, it is said, three hundred muscles into play. Place the feet close together, put the hands on the hips, rise on the toes, bend the knees and lower the body gradually till the thighs touch the heels. Extend your arms in front and fall forward, not on your nose but on your hands and toes. Keep the knees straight and body stiff, as shown in Fig. 1. Now take a piece of chalk and mark with the right hand as far as you can. Now let your companion try and do the same. By a little competition and practice, it will be found that each trial will show an improvement in the length of stretch. You should spring from the ground at a bound, and clasp your hands as you rise.

EXERCISE 20.—Stand with your feet close together and hands on hips, jump up and spread out the legs, close them, and cross them alternately.

Keep the toes pointed, or else they will come into collision with each other as they cross.

EXERCISE 21.—A pleasant feat is to jump through the hands held in front of the body, with the tips of the middle fingers together. Be careful though of your chin or your knees will catch it, which is far from pleasant; heeled shoes will also come in contact in anything but an agreeable manner with your thumbs. A variation of this is to have a staff or stick about

three feet long, and hold it with the hands about a yard apart.
Stoop down, place your knuckles on the ground in front of your
toes, holding tight the stick. Try and step over the stick
without losing your grasp or moving the knuckles from the
ground.

EXERCISE 22.—If you have a friend a few other simple exercises may be combined. Two other persons can sit down
facing each other on the floor, with the soles of their feet
touching. Then grasp a stick with their hands together, and
pull against each other; first, with the knees straight ; second,
with them bent; and thirdly, with the legs apart. Or they
may stand up facing each other, with toes opposite. Take hold
of each other's hands, lean back and go quickly round. A
third exercise with two persons, is to place the left hand on the
hips, with the right foot in front, lock the middle finger in each
other's right hand, and pull backward.

EXERCISE 23.—Minor variations of these elementary and
parlor gymnastics suggest themselves, particularly if any portion of the body is not exercised by the daily avocations.
Either arm may be advanced, and the hands turned inwards,
upwards, and outwards. Sub-rotatory and various twisting
motions of the body may be performed, the head may be turned
and twisted, and carried from side to side, the body turned
partly round at the loins, or one leg may remain stationary,
and the other moved round as far as possible on both sides.

The majority of these free movements are well adapted for
schools, and may be performed by a large number at the word
of command.

EXERCISES WITH FURNITURE.

ERE we begin with the ordinary apparatus, let us describe a
method of domestic practice, eminently adapted for the sedentary. We believe Peter Henry Ling, the author of "Kinesip-
athy ; or, Gymnastic Cures," is the generally recognised sug

gestor of these exercises, though Young Troublesome, immor
talized by Leech, had long ago brought them into domestic
practice by imitating the contortionists in the cirque at Astley's.
The chairs must, of course, be of the strong kitchen variety.

EXERCISE 24.—Place yourself between two chairs of the same
height, each hand on the back of a chair, the seats of which
are turned outwards. Rest the whole weight of the body on
both wrists, keeping the arms extended, and raise the lower
part of the body into a parallel line with the wrists. [See Fig.
20]. This position must be preserved for some seconds. Then
allow the inferior extremities to descend gradually, and return
to first position.

EXERCISE 25.—The hands on the back of the chairs, and
supporting the body by the wrists, as in the foregoing exercise.
Bend the knees and descend gently, till the knees almost touch
the ground, [See Fig. 21]. Then rise in the same manner by
the assistance of the wrists and shoulders, and return to first
position.

EXERCISE 26.—Standing between two chairs, the seats of
which are turned inwards, place a hand on each edge, keeping
the thumbs inwards, the knees bent, the feet close together,
and the heels raised. Then raise the body on the wrists, and
extend forward the lower extremities, at the same time straightening them, and thus descend gently to the ground, [See Fig.
22]. Rise again, still keeping the lower extremities extended
in front, and return to first position.

EXERCISE 27.—Placed between two chairs, the back of one
turned in and the other out, with the right hand on the back of
one and the left on the seat of the other, gently raise the lower
extremities and extend them in front ; the upper part of the
body to remain perpendicular, and supported on the wrists.
Then raise the lower extremities, bearing the whole weight of
the body on the left wrist, and place both legs on the back of
the chair by a gentle and regular impulse [See Fig. 23]. Re-

turn to the first position by the same means, and perform the same exercise on the opposite side.

EXERCISE 28.—A chair being fixed on the ground so as not to move, place both hands on the sides of its back ; then raise the body on the wrists, and elevate the lower extremities to a horizontal line, [See Fig. 24]. Allow the legs to descend gradually to the first position.

EXERCISE 29.—Two chairs being placed with the seats inwards, put the right foot between them, the left knee to be bent towards the floor, both hands fixed on the edges of the seats, and the right knee supporting the body. Then endeavor to bring the lips to the floor by extending the left knee and allowing the right to go to the floor. [See Fig. 25]. Rise by a contrary movement, and return to first position. Repeat exercise with the left side.

EXERCISE 30.—An arm-chair being placed in the middle of the room, place yourself facing the seat, with a hand on each arm of the chair, and raise the body on the wrists, at the same time raising and crossing the legs ; then pass them forward between the arms, straightening the knees, and carry them over the back of the chair without touching it. Repeat this exercise many times, until the muscles of the upper part of the body are strong enough to accomplish it with ease. [See Fig. 26].

EXERCISE 31.—(With a bench.) First place yourself upright on the bench, with the toes close together on its edge; then allow the body to descend gradually by bending the knees and supporting its weight upon them.

The elbows must be kept close to the body, the forearm extended and the fist doubled ; then rising gently return to first position, [See Fig. 27] ; repeat several times. (Second.)—Being seated across the bench or form, fix a hand on each side and raise the body on the wrists, the knees bent and raised to the height of the hips, the body to lean forward, and in this position move along the form to the end ; then make the same movement back again. [See Fig. 28].

EXERCISE 32.—Place both heels together, bend the body and knees, with the elbows close to the body ; then rising and extending the arms behind, and inclining the body forward, by means of a strong impulse, take a jump, at the same time carrying the arms forward and descending on the toes, taking care to bend the knees. Repeat many times. This exercise can be performed with very little space.

EXERCISE 33.—A table, four or five feet wide, being placed in the middle of the room, the individual stands seven or eight feet from it ; then take a run, with the right foot foremost, and when near the table, put the hands on the center of it, with the right in front and the left behind ; by a strong impulse he must then raise the body by the strength of the arms and jump to the other side of the table, with his feet together and the knees bent.

———

BALANCING.

AN essential feature in gymnastics is the preservation of the equilibrium of the body, [See Fig. 29]. If we try to balance with one hand a small stick, feather, or other object, we find how easy it is by a little judicious arrangement of a few dexterous movements to prevent it falling. If we apply the same faculties to the body, we acquire hardihood, presence of mind, and justness of eye; and a readiness at avoiding a fall by leaping. In exercising one's self in balancing, it is usual to commence standing on one leg alternately until it can be done with ease. When a man stands in an ordinary position the center of gravity passes down the spine between the feet, and of course every movement of the body changes the center of gravity ; it is never fixed. The body bends forward on one side according to the weight it bears on the other. A pole is used by professional balancers, though some of the best feats are to be done by the mere use of the arms and body without mechanical help.

After a steady balance can be kept on one leg on the ground, the gymnast passes to the edge of a brick or a pole lying on the

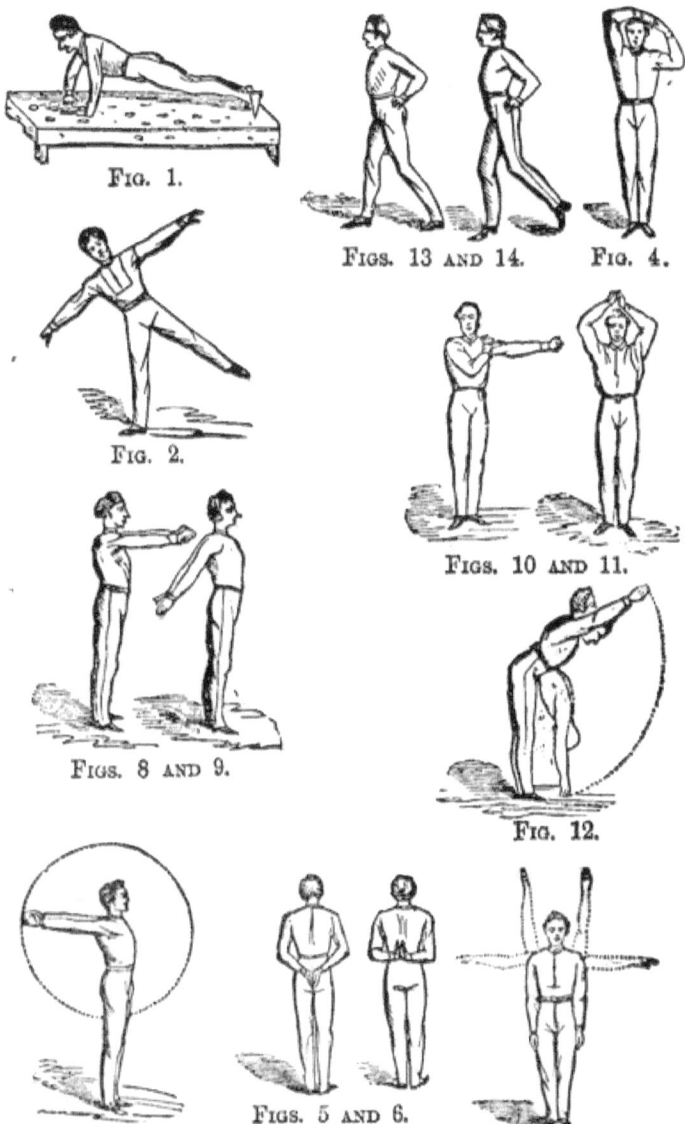

FIG. 1.

FIGS. 13 AND 14. FIG. 4.

FIG. 2.

FIGS. 10 AND 11.

FIGS. 8 AND 9.

FIG. 12.

FIG. 7.

FIGS. 5 AND 6.

FIG. 3.

ground before he mounts either the parallel or horizontal bar.
There are several ways of mounting a bar if it is no higher than
the knee or thigh: the foot is placed on it, the hands are extended in front, and the body gradually raised. Another method is
to sit astride on the bar, and with a sudden spring bring both
feet on to the bar, the feet crossing each other at the heels, at
the same time raising the body to an upright position. Unless a good balance is kept it cannot be done, [See Fig. 40,

OF THE PARALLEL BARS.

We are now out of doors, and we will try our strength and
skill on the parallel bars. They are formed of two pieces of
wood, from six to eight feet long, four inches square, rounded
at the top, so that the hand will rest on them easily. About
eighteen inches apart and four feet high will be found to be the
most convenient, but they may be fixed and varied at pleasure.

Exercise 34.—(First position, Fig. 36.) Place yourself between the bars in the center, put your hands on the right and
left bars at the same time. A slight spring will raise the body
on to the wrists. The legs must be kept close. The first position may also be obtained by an upward spring, and then place
the hands on the bars. After the wrists become accustomed
to the weight and position of the bars, try "The Walk." Use
your hands instead of your feet to move to and fro. It is not
difficult, but tiresome. It must be done regularly, with the
head above the shoulders. The weight of the body must be
kept on the rigid arm, while the other moves forward. The
Swing may next be performed. Communicate to your body a
gentle movement backwards and forwards, until it moves freely;
the knees straight, and the feet touching each other. The
swing may be increased, until in both the backward and forward movement the legs are nearly upright over the head, the
arm-sockets forming the pivot.

Exercise 35.—(Rising and Sinking.) Being in the first position, place the legs backwards, the heels close to the upper
part of the thighs. Lower yourself gently from this position,

until your elbows nearly meet behind the back. Remain in this attitude a short time, then rise gently, carefully avoiding touching the ground with your feet. You may vary this exercise by sinking gradually down as before, and kissing the bar behind each hand alternately. This is a graceful movement, but do not spoil it by touching the ground with your knees. [See Fig. 36].

EXERCISE 36.—A good and useful position is the Letter L, as it is fancifully called, [See Fig. 37.] The legs are drawn up at right angles with the body, while the knees are kept straight. It may be varied by the hands being clasped outside the bars whilst standing on the ground and forming the same figure underneath the bars

EXERCISE 37.—The gymnast will now be able to vary the preliminary exercises by throwing his legs over either bar whilst swinging [Fig. 38], and sit on the bar, or he may give himself a greater impetus and throw himself entirely over the bar on to the ground. He may proceed along the bar by a series of jumps with the hands more or less quick; or he can drop on the forearm, and let the elbow and wrist be supported by the bar, and swing in that position, [See Fig. 39]. Rise and drop into that position until it can be done surely and without effort. A nimble movement is to take the right hand from its position and to touch the left-hand bar with the right hand. Try the same movement with the left hand, and when it can be done easily try and perform the same movement by passing the hands behind the back in touching the bars.

EXERCISE 38.—Several pretty feats on the parallel bars require some little agility, but if the elementary free movements have been practiced they can easily be performed. To stand on the bars you must secure a good balance whilst astride one of the bars [See Fig. 59]. The sole of one foot may now be placed on the bar, and the toe of the other foot slipped underneath it. By means of this toe draw yourself to an upright position, and bring both feet together [See Fig 40.] To do this properly you will have to practice balancing, as before described, or you may get an ugly fall. Stand in the first position, throw one leg over each bar, and rest your hands on the bar behind the legs. Remember your swinging practice. Disengage the feet, swing boldly through the bars, and when your legs are fairly through the bars extend them and seat yourself astride with your face in the opposite direction. Swing at one end of the bars, and when in full course spring forward, catch the bars with the hands, when the body, if it is gracefully done, will be in the position of the lowered body, [See Fig. 36.] If not done carefully, beware of how you fall. The curling movement commences with the second style of the Letter L. [See Fig. 41.] Count eight or ten, then turn slowly over, keeping the knees straight until you hang in reverse. Come slowly back, until you assume the original position. Another good movement is to slide the hands forward and the legs backward; put the toes over the bars until you form the "Indian Cradle, [See Fig. 42]. This does not give a pleasant sensation. After a short interval draw yourself up again. These exercises are not necessarily performed in the order given. They may be varied almost *ad infinitum*.

CLIMBING.

EXERCISE 39.—Procure a stout board, and according to its length set it against the wall at an angle of from 30 ° to 45 °. Seize both sides of the board, place the feet flat in the center, and ascend by moving hands and feet, in short steps, alternately, [See Fig. 44.] This exercise throws great stress on the muscles of the loin and back, as well as the extensor muscles. A pole may be ascended in the same manner, but care must be taken that the shoes are not slippery. This movement can be performed in a room.

EXERCISE 40.—Procure a ladder, and raise the body by seizing hold of the rundles alternately underneath [See Fig. 44.]

Bring the elbow of the lower arm sharp to the side, previously
to pulling up the body by the other. The legs should be kept
as close as possible.

EXERCISE 41.—In climbing up a scaffold or other pole, which
may be done by grasping it by both hands, the right above the
left, the legs should alternately grasp the pole in the ascent
by means of the great toe, which is turned towards the pole,
[See Fig. 45.] In descending be careful not to come down too
fast. The friction must be thrown on the inner part of the
thighs, and the hand left comparatively free, [See Fig. 46.] In
climbing trees care should be taken to use the hands more than
the legs, and great caution should be used in laying hold of
withered branches, or they may suddenly give way. Try each
branch separately with the hands in going up, and with the
feet in going down, ere you trust your body to it.

EXERCISE 42.—Rope climbing is an excellent as well as most
useful exercise. It is comparatively easy to climb a knotted
rope, or one in which short cross pieces are inserted, but the
true gymnast despises such aids, and pulls himself up by his
hands alone, [See Fig. 47.] But ere he can attain this dexter-
ity he must make use of his feet somewhat. A sailor passes
the rope from the hands between his thighs, twists it round
one leg just below the knee and over the instep, as shown in
Fig. 48. The other foot presses on the rope, and thus a firm
hold is secured. When descending beware of letting the rope
slip, or the skin will be torn from the flesh, [See Fig. 49.] Put
one hand under another. Some clever climbers descend head
foremost, and this is by no means difficult, as the rope is held
by the feet, [See Fig. 50.]

EXERCISE 43. Seize the rope about a yard from the ground,
and run with it as far as you can. Let go and swing yourself
forward, marking the spot where the toes touch the ground ;
but this leads us to—

THE GIANT STRIDE.

This curious piece of gymnastic furniture is familiar to most schoolboys. It is like a gigantic umbrella stick, with ropes in place of the familiar whalebone and gingham. This "flying step" is generally much abused : the boys run round it instead of taking flying jumps over a ten foot pole, to set the blood aglow; and perform a series of evolutions which for grace and agility would make a poor dyspeptic patient blush for shame. The ropes attached to the revolving iron cap should be fitted with a stout cross-bar of elm or ash, about two feet in length. Hold these staffs at arms' length, and run round the pole until the whole body assumes the same line as the rope, and the feet touch the ground only at intervals. Practice this from left to right and right to left. When the plain circle can be done with ease, try a series of smaller circles with the feet whilst going round the pole. A string from the upright may be passed outside at various heights, which may be leaped by the mere action of the centrifugal force, as high as ten feet, easily by a boy. Be careful, however, not to lose your balance !

ON THE HORIZONTAL BAR.

Every one knows what a horizontal bar is, and its construction. One of the best of many modes of construction, particularly where the space is limited, is to have two strong upright posts firmly fixed in the ground, from fourteen to sixteen feet high, fitted with mortice holes to admit the horizontal bar. One of the posts should be fitted with notches to allow the gymnast to reach the top easily or to descend. [See Fig. 51.] The bar at first should be placed just out of reach of the hands of the gymnast, that a small spring is necessary to grasp it. Many of the feats on the horizontal bar here described may be performed on a swinging bar, [See Fig. 52,] as proficiency is attained. At first the bar should be firm, and the gymnast should grasp it with the hand, not with the thumb and fingers.

The thumb should rest by the side of the fingers, which should assume a hook-like form.

EXERCISE 44.—The first exercise is to hang on to the pole, the body remaining loose and straight in a natural position. Gradually let the body hang by one hand until the arms are accustomed to the weight of the body. Be cool, and do not twist, or down you will come. When the arms are used to the weight of the body, attempt to walk along the pole, moving first one hand and then the other. The body must be kept as still as possible. You may vary this by placing one hand at each side of the bar [See Fig. 53.] It will soon become easy.

EXERCISE 45.—Seize the bar with both hands and attempt to raise the body up to the bar until it is on a level with the breast [See Fig. 54.] Lower yourself gradually, and continue the exercise until it is easy and familiar. A good gymnast can do this a dozen time successively without experiencing fatigue. When it can be done easily the body may be raised to the full extent of the arm. This exerts the muscles powerfully, and requires a strong effort.

EXERCISE 46.—Now try the swing by the hands on the bar. It gives a peculiar sensation, but you soon become accustomed to it. When at the swing, accustom yourself to let go the bar and spring forward or backward on to the feet.

EXERCISE 47.—Raise the body as high as possible, throw the arms over the bar, holding firmly by them, [See Fig. 55.] This relieves the pressure on the wrists, and is a very useful exercise, particularly when the body is raised from the ground and is held up by one arm. To do this, however, the arm must be passed underneath the bar, which must be pressed firmly between the hand and shoulder [See Fig. 56.] Each arm should be tried alternately.

EXERCISE 48.—After raising yourself to the full extent of the arms, change your hands, and curl over the bar, dropping lightly on to the feet [See Fig. 57.] The changing hands is to

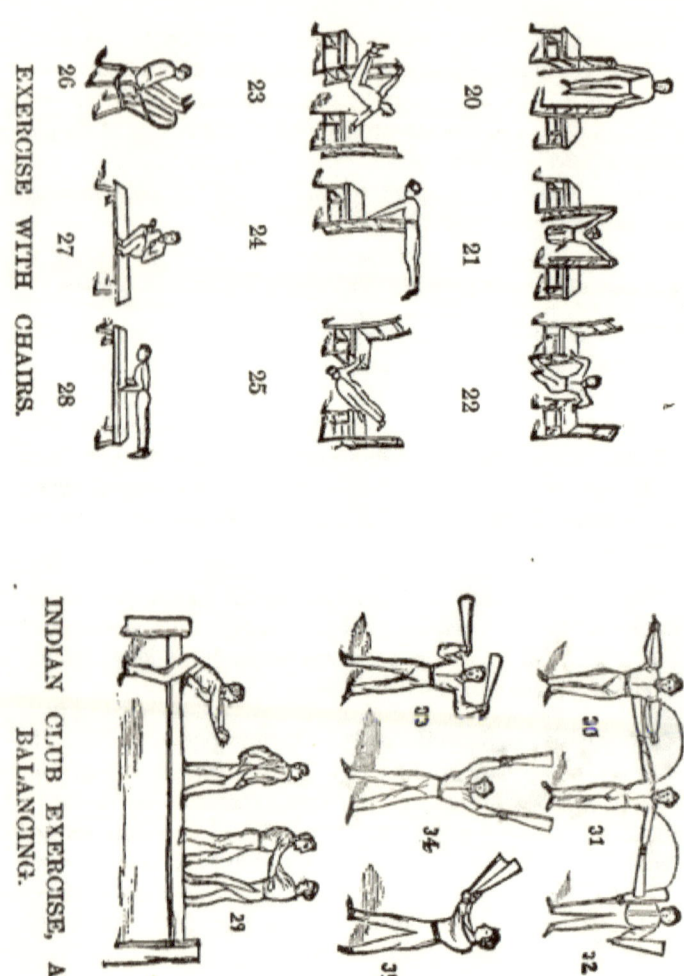

EXERCISE WITH CHAIRS.

INDIAN CLUB EXERCISE, AND BALANCING.

reverse the position of the finger points on the bar, and in this instance they must be turned towards the body.

EXERCISE 49.—(Kicking the Bar)—[See Fig. 59.] This feat is performed by hanging by the hands and drawing up the feet until the instep touches the pole. The head must be thrown well back, to counter-balance the legs and feet. Do this slowly, and beware of unnecessary jerks and strains when this can be easily accomplished.

EXERCISE 50.—May be tried. The legs are raised as in the kicking bar, but the feet are passed underneath the pole until the body hangs down with the arms twisted. The gymnast may drop on to the ground after this, or he may try to bring the body and legs back again. This will be found very difficult to all but the young and very supple. The strain on the twisted arm is very great.

EXERCISE 51.—A series of movements to sit on the bar are thus performed. When hanging on the bar, [See Fig. 53], pass one foot between the hands as in kicking the bar. Hitch the leg over the bar, the other leg must hang as low as possible. Give a swing backwards and come up right on the bar. The other leg can be brought over so as to sit on the bar [See Fig. 58.] The same attitude is often assumed by passing both feet under the bar and stretching them straight into the air until the head points to the ground, and the heels to the air. Draw yourself upwards until the weight of the legs and feet bring you upon the bar seated. In both these movements the beginner generally overbalances himself. You may leave the bar when seated on it in two ways. One of which is to put the hands on the bar with the finger points forward, slide backwards, keeping the knees bent, roll over backwards, and come down on the feet. The second is the vaulting practice. Place both hands on one side, with the fingers away from the body, then with a slight spring bring the feet over the pole and vault to the ground.

EXERCISE 52.—Hitch one leg over the bar and hold on with the hands, one on each side of the bar. Now give a swing backwards until you can give yourself such an impetus as to come right round the bar into the same position [See Fig. 60.] Try the same movement with different legs and with both hands on one side of the bar until you can do it a dozen times without stopping. The hands may be placed on each side of the bar, and the legs raised on each side and crossed above the bar, [See Figs. 61, 62.] Now try and spin round the bar like a fowl on a spit; when you can do this easily try the reverse way, bring the legs backward over the bar and spring in the Indian Cradle position, [See Fig. 63.] This is very difficult.

EXERCISE 53.—Form the Letter L, as on the parallel bars, count fifty before you drop. Bring the feet through the arms, keeping the knees straight all the time. Place one hand on each side of the bar, form Letter L, then bring the legs upwards and repeat the movement as before, but keep the arms inside the legs, as in the Fig. 64.

EXERCISE 54.—Sit on the bar, point the fingers to the front, grasp the bar firmly on each side, let your body slide forward until the bar crosses the small of the back, and the elbows project upwards. Draw yourself back again and resume the sitting position. Sit on the bar as before, then suddenly slide backwards and drop, catching yourself by your bent knees. Be careful to drop perpendicularly, and do not communicate any movement to the body. When this can be easily done, first one leg and then the other may be unhooked. The released leg may be thrown over the instep or hang loosely. When the beginner feels confidence he may hitch both insteps over the pole, forcing the toes upwards. Loosen the hands from the pole and let the body hang perpendicularly. Drop on to the ground on the hands and spring to the feet.

EXERCISE 55.—Two difficult movements are called the "trussed fowl," and the "true lover's knot." To perform the first, you hang on the bar, draw up the feet and place the in-

steps against the bar. Push the body through the arms and remain in that position as long as you can. The latter is a school-
boy's trick, and very difficult to do. Grasp the bar, pass the
left knee through the right arm until the inside of the knee
rests against the inside of the right elbow. Now pass the right
. knee over the instep of the left foot, let go the left hand, and
with it grasp the right foot. You will now hang by the right
hand in an attitude that professional tumblers can seldom
assume.

THE WOODEN HORSE.

EVERY ONE likes the exercises on the wooden horse. The apparatus is easily made. It only requires a piece of the trunk of
a tree, barked and smoothed, firmly fixed on four posts, or legs,
so that it cannot be easily pushed over. It should be the
height of the gymnast's nose. A little nearer one end than the
other, a rough, stout saddle should be placed, with the wooden
pommels covered with common leather. The hind pommel
should be rather higher than the other. On the off side of the
horse, a sawdust bed, some four feet square, should be made,
on which the gymnast may alight after he jumps. On the near
side a spring board is desirable, but not essential. A slight
covering of sand on the near side is, however, absolutely necessary to avoid slips in taking the leaps.

EXERCISE 56.—Commence by standing on the ear side of the
horse with one hand on each pommel. Spring up, bring the
arms straight, until the body is supported by the hands, and
the knees rest against the body of the horse. Spring lightly
down on the toes, and continue to practice this until it becomes
easy and natural. Then jump a little higher, throw the right
leg over the saddle, removing the hand, and you are mounted.
Practice mounting both ways. To dismount, place the left
hand on the fore pommel, and the right hand on the saddle.
A slight raising of the body, and you can throw yourself off
easily. Endeavor also to sustain the body by the hands and

arms, whilst the feet are off the ground, by throwing yourself a little way from the horse, so as to prepare yourself against the restiveness of a real nag.

EXERCISE 57.—Now then for the knees. Place your hands on the pommels, leap up and place the right knee on the saddle [See Fig. 62.] Down again, and up with the left knee on the saddle, when you can do it well and quickly by both knees, but beware of going over. To avoid this by no means uncommon occurrence, practice leaping with both knees on to the saddle, and then lean forward, make a spring and clear the legs from the saddle, and come to the ground [See Fig. 63.] Your motto in this, as in many other feats, should be "dare and do."

EXERCISE 58.—Mount and seat yourself behind the saddle. Place the left hand on the fore pommel and the right hand on the hurdle. Swing the body completely round, so as to seat yourself before the saddle. Change hands, and bring yourself into the position from which you started. You may vary this as follows : When mounted, place both hands on the front pommel. Swing yourself as high in the air as you can. Cross both legs whilst doing so, and twist the body so as to seat yourself again on the saddle, but looking in the opposite direction. Try the reverse action, and resume your original position. This is more astonishing than useful. Other feats are performed on the horse,—as vaulting, leaping on to the saddle with one hand on the pommels, and turning somersaults over the saddle, jumping through the arms [See Figs. 64 and 65,] leaping on to the horse as if it had a side-saddle on [See Fig. 66 ;] but these do not require any special directions. Fig. 67 represents the back vault.

LEAPING AND VAULTING.

EXERCISE 59.—Leaping was a favorite exercise of the Greeks, and is one of the most useful of the gymnastic exercises. It admits of great variety. There is the standing jump, the

jump over the hurdle, bar rod, string, or cat-gallows. Leapers
raise the feet and knees in the straight direction, not separating
the legs. The body should be inclined forward, the run not
too long, and in coming to the ground the fall should not be on
the heels, but on the toes and soles of the feet. This is of
great importance. Unaided by a pole or other implement, a
man can jump at best something short of his own height. In
a low jump the knees are raised with the spring of the body,
but in higher leaps the legs must be kept well under the body.
In leaping from a height the balance should be well preserved,
as there is a tendency to come down on the nose. In leaping
upwards the body must be kept well forward, as there is a tendency in this instance to fall backwards. In long leaps, the
inexperienced generally throw the body over, instead of jumping feet foremost and recovering their balance by the spring of
the body.

VAULTING.

EXERCISE 60.--To vault with grace and agility is a nice and
useful accomplishment. The hands should be placed on the
object, and the body and the legs thrown over it, as illustrated
by the exercises on the wooden horse. Vaulters can throw
themselves over a height of five feet six inches to six feet.

Pole leaping is now becoming much in vogue. The pole
should be strong enough to bear the weight of the leaper without bending, and sound enough not to fracture at the critical
moment. The pole for beginners need not be more than seven
feet long, and an attempt should be made to spring short dis-
tances with it. The hands should not be placed higher than
the head, the right hand at the top, and the left hand may be
placed in the most convenient position. The spring must be
taken from the left foot at the instant the pole touches the
ground, and a short run may be taken to give the necessary
impetus. Now, in our school-days, we always held the pole
until the ground was reached, and of course came down with

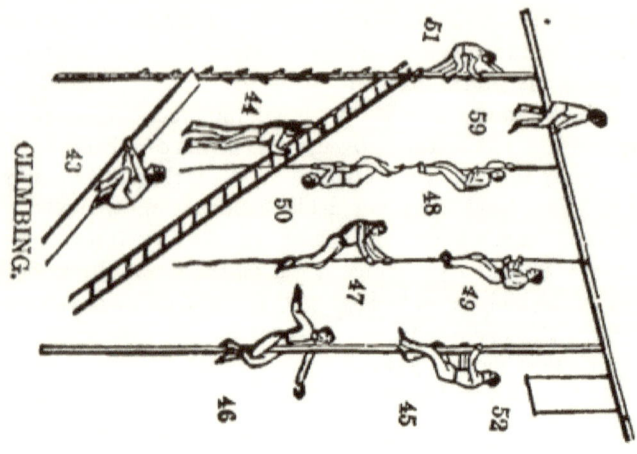

CLIMBING.

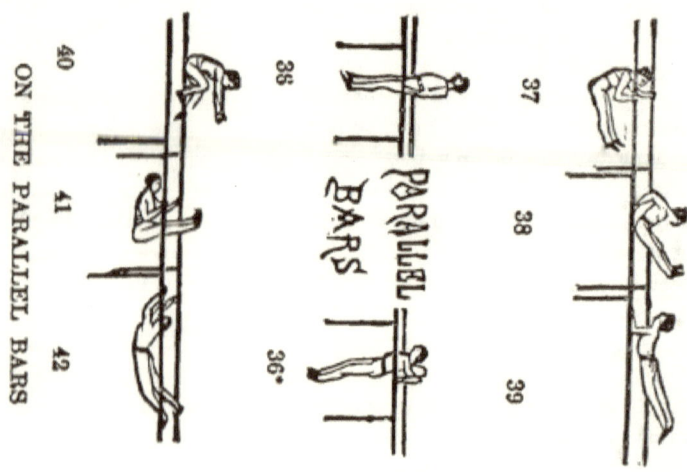

ON THE PARALLEL BARS

our face towards the spot from whence we started. But since that period high and perpendicular leaps are taken over a six-feet and higher bar, and the pole is left behind. Care must be taken to place the hands high enough, and to have the end of the pole pointed, so that it will remain sticking in the ground. By letting the pole go as the body goes over the bar, the leaper descends straight forwards as in an ordinary jump. When you loose the bar, push it behind so as to make it fall backwards. As the leaper goes over the bar, the knees must be bent, so that on touching the ground they will form a spring, and the force of the fall is broken.

With a light pole and low jump, it is sometimes carried over. In long leaps, as much as eight or ten yards may be cleared Leaps from a height may be practiced, always bearing in mind that the pole must bear your weight, and that on reaching the ground the knees be bent for the spring.

If these directions are followed, you may attain health and agility though you may not attain the skill of leaping over a bar upwards of eleven feet in height, or emulate the professional gymnast on the "bar," "wooden horse," or "swing poles."

THE A. B. C. OF SWIMMING.

THE USES OF SWIMMING.

WE need scarcely say that every one ought to know how to swim. There is not a man, woman, or child in the country that cannot, and ought not to learn how to swim. There is no absolute necessity for learning the various aquatic tricks which are performed by masters and mistresses of the art, but there is a necessity that all should know how to support themselves in the water.

There is, perhaps, no athletic exercise which is so easily learned, which is so well adapted to both sexes of all ages, and yet so little known.

HOW TO BEGIN.

THE first care of the intending swimmer is, of course, to find a proper piece of water in which to learn his first lessons. The very best water that can be found is that of the sea, on account of its saltness and bitterness, whereby two great advantages are obtained.

The first advantage is, that, on account of the salt and other substances which are dissolved in it, the sea water is so much heavier than fresh, that it gives more support to the body, and enables the beginner to float much sooner than he can expect to do in fresh water.

The other advantage is, that the taste of the sea water is so nauseous that the learner takes very good care to keep his lips tightly shut, and so does not commit the common error of opening the mouth, which is fatal to all swimming, and is sure to dishearten a beginner by letting water get down his throat and half choke him.

As to place, there is nothing better than a sloping sandy shore, where the tide is not very strong. In some places the tide runs with such force, that if the beginner is taken off his legs, he will be carried away, or at least that he will have great difficulty in regaining his feet.

We strongly recommend him to walk over the spot at low water, and see whether there are any stones, sticks, rocks, or holes, and if so, to remove all the moveable impediments and mark the position of the others.

Take especial care of the holes, for there is nothing so treacherous. A hole of some six or seven inches in depth and a yard in diameter, looks so insignificant when the water is out that few persons would take any notice of it. But, when a novice is in the water, these few inches make just the difference between safety and death.

On sandy shores, the most fertile source of holes is to be found in large stones. They sink rather deeply into the sand and form minature rocks, round which the water courses as the tides ebb and flow, thus cutting a channel completely round the stone. Even when the stone is removed, the hole will remain unfilled throughout several tides.

The next best place for learning to swim is the river with a fine sandy bed, clear water, and no weeds. Since that extraordinary river weed has sweep throughout our canals and rivers, it is extremely difficult to find a stream that is free from weeds. However, it will be easy enough to. clear a sufficient space in which a learner can take his first lessons.

When such a spot has been found, the next care is to examine the bed of the river and to remove very carefully everything that might hurt the feet. If bushes should grow on the banks, look out carefully for broken scraps of boughs, which fall into the stream, become saturated with water, sink to the bottom, and become fixed with one of the points upwards.

If human hibitations should be near, beware of broken glass and crockery, fragments of which are generally thrown into the river, and will inflict most dangerous wounds if trodden on. If the bed of the stream should be in the least muddy, look for mussels, which lie imbedded almost to their sharp edges, that project upwards and cut the feet nearly as badly as broken glass.

Failing sea or river, a pond or canal is the only resource, and furnishes the very worst kind of water. The bed of most ponds is studded with all kinds of cutting and piercing objects, which are thrown in by careless boys and remain where they fell. Then, the bottom is almost invariably muddy, and the water is seldom clean. Still, bad as is a pond, it is better than nothing and the intending swimmer may console himself with the reflection that he is doing his duty, and with the prospect of swimming in the sea some time or other.

Of course, the large public baths possess some of the drawbacks of ponds, but they have at all events the advantage of a regulated depth, a firm bank, and no mud.

CONFIDENCE THE ESSENCE OF SWIMMING.

As THE very essence of swimming lies in confidence, it is always better for the learner to feel secure that he can leave the water whenever he likes. Therefore, let him take a light rope of tolerable length, tie one end to some firm object on the bank, and let the rest of the rope lie in the water. Manilla is the best kind of rope for this purpose, because it is so light that it floats on the surface instead of sinking, as is the case with an ordinary hempen rope.

If there is only sand on the shore, the rope can be moored quite firmly by tying it to the middle of a stout stick, burying the stick a foot or so in the sand and filling up the trench. You may pull till you break the rope, but you will never pull the stick out of its place. If you are very nervous, tie two sticks in the shape of a cross and bury them in like manner.

The rope need not be a large one, as it will not have to sustain the whole weight of your body, and it will be found that a cord as thick as an ordinary washing line will answer every purpose.

On the side of a stream or pond, tie the rope to a tree, or hammer a stake in the ground. A stake eighteen inches in length, and as thick as an ordinary broomstick, is quite large enough. Hammer it rather more than two-thirds into the ground, and let it lean boldly away from the water's edge. The best way of fixing the rope to it is by the " clove hitch."

Now, having your rope in your hand, go quietly into the water backwards, keeping your face towards the bank. As soon as you are fairly in the water, duck completely beneath the surface. Be sure that you do go fairly under water, for there is nothing more deceptive than the feel of water to a novice. He dips his head, as he fancies, at least a foot beneath the surface ; he feels the water in his nose, he hears it in his ears, and thinks that he is almost at the bottom, when, in reality, the back of his head is quite dry.

The best way of "ducking" easily is to put the left hand on the back of the head, hold to the rope with the right hand, and then duck until the left hand is well under water.

The learner should next accustom himself to the new element by moving about as much as possible, walking as far as the rope will allow him, and jumping up and down so as to learn by experience the buoyancy of the water.

Perhaps the first day may be occupied by this preliminary process, and on the second visit the real business may begin.

NECESSITY FOR A GOOD BEGINNING.

In swimming as in most other pursuits, a good beginning is invaluable. Let the learner bestow a little care on the preliminaries, and he will have no bad habits to unteach himself afterwards. It is quite easy to learn a good style at first as a bad style, although the novice may just at the beginning fancy that he could do better by following his own devices.

The first great object is to feel a perfect confidence in the sustaining power of the water, and according to our ideas, the best method of doing so is by learning to float on the back.

We will give a separate paragraph to the important point of floating on the back :

To take care that the cord is within easy reach, so that it may be grasped in a moment, should the novice become nervous, as he is rather apt to do just at first. Take it in both hands, and lay yourself very gently in the water, arching the spine backwards as much as possible, and keeping the legs and knees perfectly straight and stiff.

Now, press the head as far back as possibly can be done, and try to force the back of the head between the shoulder blades. You can practice this attitude at home, by lying on two chairs and seeing whether your attitude corresponds with that which is given in the illustration.

When you have thus lain in the water you will find that you are almost entirely upheld by its sustaining power, and that only a very little weight laid in the water. On reflection, you will also discern that the only weight which pulls on the rope is that of your hands and arms, which are out of water, and which, therefore, act as dead weight.

Indeed, you might just as well lay several iron weights of a pound each upon your body, for the hands and arms are much heavier than we generally fancy. Just break an arm or a leg, and you will find out what heavy articles they are.

Now, let your arms sink gradually into the water, and you will see that exactly in proportion as they sink, so much weight is taken off the rope ; and if you have only courage to put them entirely under water, and to loose the rope, your body will be supported by the water alone.

These are facts, but we may as well have reasons.

Bulk for bulk, a human being weighs considerably less than water, i. e., at the temperature of ordinary sea or river water. Now, as the lighter substance will float in the denser, it follows that the human body will float in water. If a dead body be flung into the water, some part of it will float above the surface until the lungs get choked up with water, and so the whole body is much heavier than it ought to be.

Now, supposing that a living person in a fainting condition, and, therefore, unable to struggle, were to fall into the water some part of the body would remain above the surface. But as the head, which is one solid mass of brain, muscle, and bone, is much heavier than water, it follows that the head would hang down in the water, and the shoulder-blades would appear above the surface, being buoyed up by the air-filled lungs. The hands and arms, of course, follow their natural inclination, and fall forward, thus turning the body on its face.

Then this is the natural position of a living human being in the water, provided that he does not attempt to struggle or alter his position. And the knowledge of this fact is the key to all swimming on scientific principles.

A considerable part of the body remains above the water, but it is the wrong part, as far as the preservation of life is concerned. We want to breathe, and it is very clear that we cannot breathe through our shoulders. Therefore, the first point in swimming is to reverse the natural order of things, and to bring the nostrils above the surface of the water.

The mouth may be set aside altogether, because there is no

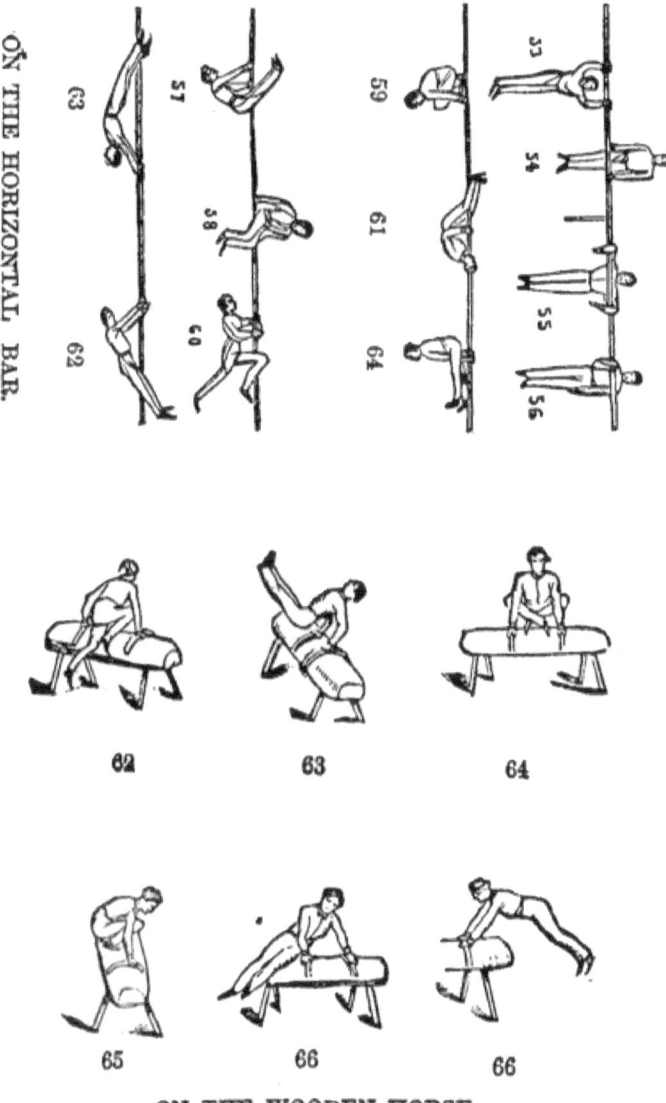

ON THE HORIZONTAL BAR.

ON THE WOODEN HORSE.

necessity for that apperture in swimming. It is meant for eating and for talking, but was never intended for breathing, which is the only function a swimmer regards.

Swimming, therefore, resolves itself into the ability to keep the nostrils above water, and the difficulty lies in the fact the nostrils are set in the heaviest part of the whole body, and that which is absolutely certain to sink below the surface unless continual efforts are being made to keep it in its right position.

On looking at the illustration it is evident that the simplest method of obtaining this object is to reverse the entire position of the body. Let, therefore, the learner be on his back, let him arch the spine in directly the opposite direction, and bend the head backwards instead of letting it hang forwards.

The result of this change of posture will be at once apparent. The heaviest part of the body, the back of the head, will be partly supported by the water, and partly by the air which fills the lungs. The nostrils will then become the lightest part of the body, and will, of course, be above the surface when the remainder is submerged.

Practically, the bather will find this result. If he will assume the attitude which has been thus described, and will be content to keep his lips tightly shut, and his limbs perfectly still, he will find that when he takes an inspiration the face will rise almost entirely out of the water. At each expiration the face will sink as far as the eyebrows and the lower lip, but no farther, the nostrils being always left free for the passage of air to the lungs.

Any one who will give this plan a fair trial will gain more real knowledge of swimming in an hour than can be obtained in a year by mere practical teaching. So powerful is the buoyancy of the water that if any one, whether he can swim or not, will lie in the attitude that has been described, and will not stir hand or foot, he cannot sink if he tries. A cork will sink as soon as he.

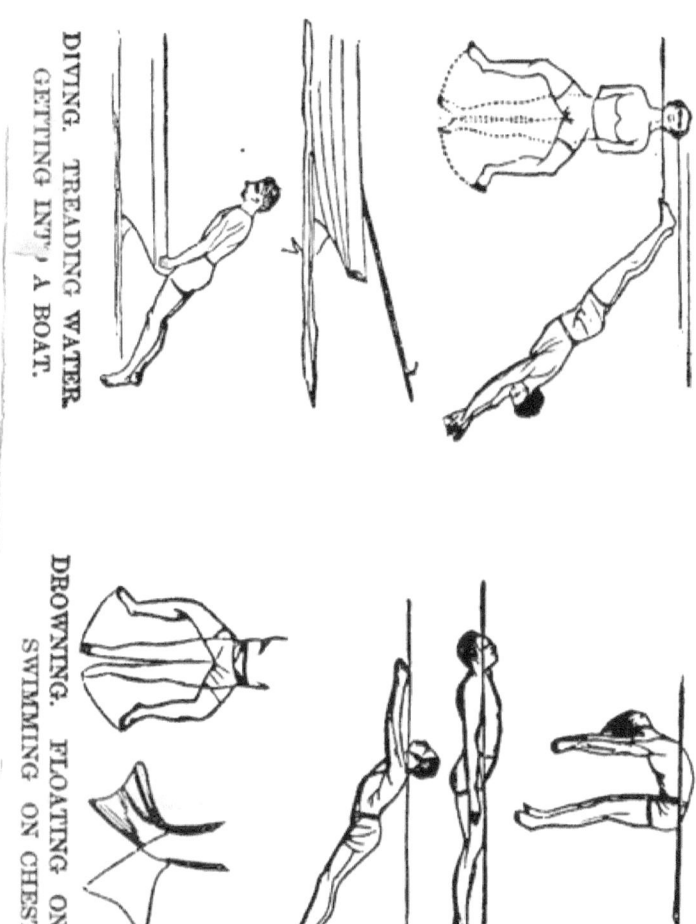

DIVING. TREADING WATER. GETTING INTO A BOAT.

DROWNING. FLOATING ON BACK. SWIMMING ON CHEST.

THE SIDE STROKE.

WE now come to that particular stroke which, in our opinion, and in that of most professional swimmers, is by far the most valuable.

This is the celebrated side stroke, so called because the swimmer lies on his side.

There is no stroke that enables the swimmer to last so long as it does, and for this reason: instead of employing both arms and legs simultaneously in the same manner, the side stroke employs them simultaneously but in different manners; so that when the swimmer is tired of exercising one side he can just turn over and proceed with the other, the change of action resting the limbs almost as much as repose would do. Mr. Beckwith, the ex-champion of England, who held the belt for so many years, always employed the side stroke when swimming his matches, and the present champion follows his example. Indeed, out of all the professionals, there is scarcely one in twenty who adopts the old-fashioned breast stroke.

The side stroke is thus managed.

The swimmer lies on his right side, stretching his right arm out as far as he can reach, keeping the fingers of the right hand quite straight and the hand itself held edgewise, so as to cut the water like a shark's fin. The left hand is placed across the chest, with the back against the right breast, and the swimmer is then ready to begin.

He commences by making the usual stroke with his legs, and the right leg, being undermost, doing the greater share of the work. Before the impetus gained by the stroke is quite expended, the right arm is brought round with a broad sweep, until the palm of the hand almost touches the right thigh. At the same moment, the left hand makes a similar sweep, but is carried backwards as far as it can go.

The reader will see that the hands act directly upon the water like the blades of a pair of oars, and do not waste any of their power by oblique action.

In ordinary swimming we seldom use the left arm, but allow

it to hang quietly in the water, so that it may be perfectly ready for work when wanted. Then, after some little time, we turn round, swim on the other side, and give the left arm its fair share of labor.

There is a modification of swimming on the side, which is sometimes called thrusting, and sometimes the Indian stroke, because the North American Indians generally employ it.

These terms are rather vaguely employed, but the former is generally used when the swimmer thrusts his arm forward, and the latter when he swings it.

In performing this stroke, the swimmer starts upon his right side, and sweeps his right hand through the water as above mentioned. While that arm is passing through the water, the left arm is swung just above the surface with a bold sweep, the hand dipping into the water when the arm is stretched to its utmost. This movement brings the body over to the left side when the two hands change duties, the left being swept under the body while the right is swung forward.

This is rather a showy style of swimming, but we do not think very much of it. It certainly propels the swimmer with great rapidity for a time, but it requires so much exertion that he is sure to tire before very long. We recollect seeing a race for a silver cup, in which the merits and defects of this stroke were well shown. The swimmer shot ahead of all his competitors with ease, and if the course had been a short one, he would quickly have won.

But the course was a tolerably long one, and the consequence was that when he had traversed almost half the distance, his exertions began to tell on him, and his strokes got rather wild and irregular. Before very long some of the steadier swimmers began to creep up to him, and before two-thirds of the distance was traversed he was passed by two of them. The result of the race was, although he was well ahead half way, he did not even get a place at the finish.

———

NEW AND POPULAR BOOKS.

TRICKS AND DIVERSIONS WITH CARDS.

An entirely new work, containing all the Tricks and Deceptions with Cards ever invented, including the latest tricks of the most celebrated Conjurers, Magicians and Prestidigitators, popularly explained, simplified and adapted for Home Amusement and Social entertainments. They are so elucidated that any one with a little practice, can perform the most difficult tricks, to his own satisfaction and to the wonder and admiration of his friends. There is also a complete exposure of all the Card Tricks made use of by Professional Card Players, Blacklegs and Gamblers. It also contains the art of Fortune Telling by Cards. Illustrated by many engravings.—*Price, 30 Cents.*

THE MAGICIAN'S GUIDE; OR, CONJURING MADE EASY.

A complete Manual of Instruction in the art of Magic, by a celebrated Professional. This book will be largely sought for by all who desire to become acquainted with the Mysteries of Magic, and to make their mark in social amusements or public entertainments. This book is not a compilation of disconnected experiments, but a regular systematic course of instruction, beginning at the simplest feats of Legerdemain, and, by a series of progressive lessons, takes the learner into the more complicated operations of Natural Magic, Chemistry, Galvanism, Magnetism, and Electricity. It is the only work published that really teaches the Conjuror's Art. Illustrated by numerous engravings.—*Price, 25 Cents.*

THE GREAT CHINESE WIZARD'S HAND-BOOK OF MAGIC.

A book of Marvels. The Mysteries of the Black Art are now exposed. The mysteries and awe-inspiring feats and performances of the most celebrated Magicians, Enchanters and Wizards are here explained, including the operations of Conjurors of Ancient and Modern times. The most amazing and apparently most wonderful impossibilities in Natural Magic, Chemistry, Galvanism, Electricity, Cards, Jugglery, Coins, Ledgerdemain, White Magic, &c., are made quite clear, so that any one can perform them. It also contains the art of making Fire Works.—*Price, 20 Cents*

RIDDLES, CONUNDRUMS AND PUZZLES.

The choicest, newest and best collection of Riddles, Conundrums, Charades, Enigmas, Anagrams, Rebusses, Transpositions, Puzzles, Problems, Paradoxes, Acrostics and other entertaining matter, ever published. For Children of all Growths. Here is Fun for the Mirthful, Food for the Curious, and Matter for the Thoughtful.—*Price, 20 Cents.*

Sent to any address by mail, post paid, on receipt of price.